HERBIE JONES AND THE MONSTER BALL

"Herbie and his friend, Raymond, who have just completed the third grade, plan to spend the summer fishing. When Herbie's Uncle Dwight, a star college baseball player, comes to town to coach the eight-and-nine-year-old team, Raymond signs the boys up, even though they are both "instant outs" in school. Then, with a little detective work and the help of the class know-it-all, Annabelle Louisa Hodgekiss, the boys jump to the conclusion that Uncle Dwight is marrying their teacher, Miss Pinkham. Readers will laugh along with Herbie as he solves his problems in typical third grade fashion."

—*School Library Journal* (Starred review)

Herbie Jones
and the **Monster Ball**

Herbie Jones
and the Monster Ball

by Suzy Kline

illustrated by Richard Williams

Puffin Books

Acknowledgments
Special appreciation to the three
people who help me think things
through—my editor, Anne O'Connell,
my husband, Rufus, and my mother,
Martha Weaver.

PUFFIN BOOKS
A Division of Penguin Books USA Inc.
375 Hudson Street, New York, New York 10014
Penguin Books Ltd, 27 Wrights Lane, London W8 5TZ, England
Penguin Books Australia Ltd, Ringwood, Victoria, Australia
Penguin Books Canada Ltd., 10 Alcorn Avenue, Toronto, Ontario, Canada M4V 3B2
Penguin Books (N.Z.) Ltd, 182–190 Wairau Road, Auckland 10, New Zealand

Penguin Books Ltd, Registered Offices: Harmondsworth, Middlesex, England

First published in the United States of America by G. P. Putnam's Sons, 1988
Published in Puffin Books, 1990
9 10 8
Text copyright © Suzy Kline, 1988
Illustrations copyright © Richard Williams, 1988
All rights reserved

LIBRARY OF CONGRESS CATALOGING IN PUBLICATION DATA
Kline, Suzy.   Herbie Jones and the monster ball / Suzy Kline ;
pictures by Richard Williams.   p.   cm.
Reprint. Originally published: New York : Putnam, c1988.
Summary: Strike-out king, Herbie Jones, feels that this summer is
ruined when his uncle arrives to coach a baseball team and asks Herbie to join up.
ISBN 0-14-034170-6
[1. Baseball—Fiction. 2. Uncles—Fiction.] I. Williams,
Richard, 1950–   ill. II. Title.
PZ7.K6797Hi 1990   [Fic]—dc20   89-10595

Printed in the United States of America
Set in Caledonia

For Uncle Doug Kline—
a baseball great

Thank you for giving six wonderful
years to our family life, and for
helping Rufus coach Jennifer and
Emily in the golden years of the
A's, Royals, and Yankees.

Contents

1

A Knock at Midnight

Raymond Martin peeked out of his sleeping bag. "I'm starved, Herbie," he said.

Herbie Jones rolled over and stuck his head out of his sleeping bag. "What?" he moaned.

"Can we get something to eat in your house?"

Herbie moaned and groaned some more. Then he unzipped his sleeping bag. "It's late, Ray, but come on. We just have to be real quiet. I don't want to wake up Mom or Olive."

"You're lookin' at Captain Tiptoe," Ray replied with a toothy grin.

The boys ran across the backyard and entered the backdoor quietly. They tiptoed into the kitchen and opened the refrigerator door.

"Where's the food?" Ray asked as the refrigerator light went on.

"You're lookin' at it," Herbie replied with a yawn.

Ray leaned forward. "What are those moldy looking golf balls?"

"Those are brussels sprouts with cheese sauce."

Ray made a face.

"How about that?" Ray said pointing to a bowl with foil over it.

Herbie removed the foil. "Oh, those are leftovers from last night's dinner."

Ray looked at them closely. "I can see why they were left over."

Herbie closed the refrigerator door. "So, have a cracker," he said handing his buddy a package of saltines.

Ray wolfed them down.

Then in the middle of his chomping, he stopped. "Do you hear something?"

"Yeah," Herbie replied. "You eating."

"No . . . the knocking noise."

Herbie listened. "I don't hear anything," he said.

"Listen again," Ray whispered.

Herbie didn't move. There *was* a knock at the door. Herbie's eyes widened.

"Do you think it's the mailman?" Ray asked.

"No, dummy," Herbie whispered. "No one delivers the mail at midnight."

"That's what I thought," Ray whispered back. "They're probably afraid of the dark too."

Herbie didn't say anything. He just walked very quietly to the front door.

Ray put his crackers on the table and followed him.

The moonlight illuminated the living room just enough so the boys could find their way without bumping into furniture.

"Down on your knees," Herbie whispered.

Ray got down. The two of them crawled to the front window. Slowly, Herbie moved the curtain to one side.

Both boys stared at the front porch.

No one was there.

Herbie stood up in relief. "There was no knock at the door. We're both dreaming! Let's get back to bed."

The boys went back outside and crawled into their sleeping bags.

A few minutes later, Ray whispered, "Herbie?"

"Now what? I'm sleeping."

"There *is* someone knocking at the door. It's the backdoor now and I can see him!"

Herbie sat up. He saw a tall dark figure knocking on the screen door. "You're sure right, Ray," Herbie whispered.

"He doesn't have a mailbag either," Ray said as he yanked the sleeping bag over his head.

Herbie watched the dark figure knock again and then turn. Herbie wondered if the stranger saw him.

"Someone there?" the stranger called out.

Ray shivered in his sleeping bag. "I'm never sleeping over at your house again, Herbie Jones. It's too dangerous! You don't even have a dog like my Shadow to protect you!"

Herbie kept his eyes on the stranger. He decided to ask him who he was looking for.

"What do you want?" Herbie said in a squeaky voice, "and who *are* you?"

The stranger spoke up right away. "DWIGHT JONES."

Herbie paused for a minute and then he shot out of his sleeping bag. "UNCLE DWIGHT!"

Not a Murderer

"Uncle Dwight! Uncle Dwight!" Herbie yelled as he ran into his arms.

"HERBIE! How are you, boy?"

After the two hugged, Dwight looked at his nephew and tousled his hair. "I hope I didn't scare you and your friend."

"Nah, we weren't afraid. Ray! You can come out now!"

Raymond peeked his head out of his sleeping bag. Slowly, he joined Herbie on the porch. "You're not a thief or a murderer?"

"No, I'm just Herbie's uncle."

"Oh." Ray put his hands in his pajama pockets and stood behind Herbie.

"Uncle Dwight, this is my buddy, Raymond Martin. He's got the biggest baseball card collection at school."

"Always nice to meet a baseball fan, Raymond," Dwight said, holding out his hand.

"He wants to shake hands, Ray," Herbie coaxed.

Ray stuck out his hand and shook hands with Herbie's uncle.

"Well," Herbie said, "come on in."

As Herbie turned on the kitchen light, he took a good look at his uncle. His head almost touched the top of the doorway. He was so tall! His dad always talked a lot about his youngest brother Dwight. Herbie was even named after him—Herbert Dwight Jones.

Uncle Dwight was a junior at the University of Connecticut and he played first base.

"When will you be playing baseball on TV?" Herbie asked.

Uncle Dwight laughed. "Well, I have to be drafted by the majors first. I have one more season to play ball at the University."

"Hungry?" Herbie asked.

"Starved," Dwight said, opening the re-frigerator. "What are those moldy looking golf balls?"

Ray stepped away from Herbie and toward Uncle Dwight. "You and me are gonna get along fine," he said. "Here, have a cracker."

Suddenly, Mrs. Jones and Olivia appeared at the kitchen door. "What are you boys doing up in the middle of the night?" Then she saw Dwight. "Dwight Jones—You rascal you!"

And she ran across the kitchen to give him a hug. "Why didn't you let us know you were coming?"

"You know me, Mary. Last-minute Dwight. I meant to call you this time. I knew I was coming but . . ."

". . . you just couldn't get to the phone," Mrs. Jones finished. "Well, it sure is great to see you. Where are your bags?"

Uncle Dwight snapped his fingers. "Did I leave them at the bus station? No, I had them when I walked over here."

Mrs. Jones shook her head.

"They're on the grass with the Monster Ball," Uncle Dwight finally remembered.

Mrs. Jones smiled.

Ray stood behind Herbie again. "Wh . . . wh . . . what's a Monster Ball?" he whispered.

"Tell you later," Herbie replied.

Then Uncle Dwight spotted Olivia. She was standing in the doorway in her long, pink bathrobe. Her hair was all gnarled.

"And who is *this* beauty?" he asked as he held out his arms.

Olivia ran to her uncle and he lifted her up high. She put her sleepy head on his shoulder. "How long can you stay this time?" she asked.

"Well," he said, putting her down, "my coach got me a job in Laurel Woods. Apparently they need a recreation director for the summer."

"All summer! Wow!" Herbie shouted.

"So, until I get called back to baseball camp," Uncle Dwight said, "this will be my home—if that's okay."

Mrs. Jones beamed. "Your brother will sure be happy to see you. Your room in the attic is always waiting for you. The bed's still unmade—just the way you left it last Christmas."

Uncle Dwight laughed loudly.

"I better wash the sheets tomorrow," she added.

As Herbie and Ray walked across the yard to

their sleeping bags, Herbie put his arm around his buddy. "This is gonna be our best summer yet."

In the morning, Herbie felt the warm sun on his face. When he rolled over to check on Raymond, he saw an empty sleeping bag.

Where was he?

Herbie ran barefoot across the lawn. As he peered in through the backdoor window, he saw Ray at the kitchen table with his uncle, father, and Olivia, eating pancakes.

Herbie opened the door.

"I'd love seconds," Ray said as Mrs. Jones piled another stack on his plate.

"Morning, Herbie!" Mr. Jones called out. He had just gotten home a half hour ago from his nightshift at Northeastern Factory. "What do you think about your ol' uncle spending the summer, huh?"

And then he jabbed his brother in the side.

"It's great!" Herbie said as he sat down at the table next to Uncle Dwight. "Dad, do you think I'll get to be as tall as Uncle Dwight?"

"Maybe. Aunt Martha was six feet."

"Six feet?" Olivia shrieked. "If I'm that tall, I'll just die." And then she turned to her mother. "Promise me, Mom, I won't be six feet."

Mrs. Jones looked at her husband and then at Uncle Dwight. She needed help.

"Well," Uncle Dwight said, "I like my women tall."

Olivia managed a smile. Her uncle's opinion was important.

Mrs. Jones decided it was time to change the subject.

"So, when do you start your new job?"

Uncle Dwight's face turned red. "Actually, I start today."

"Today?" Mrs. Jones exclaimed.

"I meant to get here earlier but I had a lot of junk to clean out of my apartment."

Herbie thought about his uncle's room in the attic and how much junk he had in there!

"Anyway," Uncle Dwight said as he gulped down some milk, "the job sounds great. They're starting an eight- and nine-year-old baseball league in town and all the parks are participating. Did you guys know about it?"

Herbie did. He wanted no part of it.

Ray spoke up right away. "Sure, we were even thinkin' of signing up."

Herbie shot Ray a dirty look. How could he say something like that, he thought.

"Well, one of the things I'll be doing," Uncle Dwight continued, "is coaching the team from Laurel Woods!"

Herbie dropped his napkin on his plate.

"Looks like we'll be spending some time together guys, playing ball!"

Herbie picked up the pitcher of maple syrup and poured it over his napkin.

Mr. Jones broke out laughing. "Herbie's so excited about baseball he can't tell the difference between a napkin and a pancake!"

Herbie tried to smile but it was hard.

"Well," Ray replied, "you know how it is around here. Me and Herbie are known as Mr. Baseball."

Herbie started to eat the soggy napkin.

"Yeah," Ray continued, "everyone calls us the Touchdown Twins at school."

"Touchdown Twins?" Olivia made a face. "That's football, not baseball!"

"Well," Ray added, swallowing a mouthful of pancakes, "we're great at that, too."

The conversation was making Herbie sick.

"Okay, you two Sluggers, it's settled. See you at the park at 9:30 for the team sign-up. The first practice starts today!"

"I'm glad you can coach Herbie, Dwight," Mr. Jones said. "I never get a chance to work with him. I have to sleep all day."

Suddenly Mr. Jones had a thought. He got up from the table and opened the kitchen door to the attic. "Be back in a minute."

When the door opened again, Mr. Jones was standing there with a baseball glove. "This used to belong to me when I was a kid. Then Dwight used it in high school. Lots of fly balls ended up in this baby," Mr. Jones said, pounding the pocket. "Now, it's yours, Herbie! Catch!"

Herbie jumped up from the table and tried to grab it but he missed.

The mitt slipped out of his hand and landed in the butter dish.

"Eeyew!" Olivia sounded. "Look at it *now*."

Uncle Dwight picked the mitt off the table. A big chunk of margarine was hanging from it.

"Hey, Slugger," he said, tossing the mitt to Herbie. "You'll have to do a *butter* job of catching than that!"

Mr. Jones and Uncle Dwight roared.

"Way to go, Erb," Olivia clapped her hands. "It's old butterfingers himself!"

Herbie ran to the bathroom.

3

The Death Scene

When Mr. Jones went off to bed, Mrs. Jones and Olivia went grocery shopping. It was Mrs. Jones's day off. "You can do the dishes later," she said to Olivia as they walked out the door.

Raymond remained at the table. He was busy finishing the leftover pancakes from other people's plates. After he did that, he scraped the butter off the mitt with his finger and popped it in his mouth.

Then he went looking for Herbie.

Herbie was still in the bathroom.

Raymond knocked. "You okay, Herbie?"

"No."

"What's wrong?"

"I'm dying."

"Dying?"

Herbie opened the door a crack. "Yeah, I ate a napkin."

"That's nothing," Ray replied. "I read in the newspaper some guy ate a box of Kleenex. You'll be okay."

It was quiet for a moment.

"So what happened to the guy who ate the box of Kleenex?"

"He had to find something else to put his tissues in."

Herbie opened the door wide. "That was not funny. I suppose you made it up."

Ray made a toothy grin. "I thought it was good."

Herbie staggered to his bed and then plopped down on it. "I don't have much time," he said in a faint voice. "That napkin is in my blood stream now, on its way to my heart."

"Stop it!" Ray shouted.

Herbie sat up. "Shhh! You'll wake my dad." Then he dropped back to the bed and closed his eyes again.

"Herbie Jones," Ray said as he lifted one of Herbie's eyelids, "you are a big phoney. You're not dying. You just don't want to sign up for your uncle's baseball team."

Herbie sat up and poked Ray in the chest. "*You* are the phoney! We never thought about signing up for this baseball league. We were gonna fish all summer, remember?"

"Fish and spy," Ray corrected.

"So how could you have such a big mouth? Now my uncle thinks we're baseball greats. BASE-BALL GREATS—that's funny! You hit nubbers that roll three feet and I strike out all the time. We're INSTANT OUTS at school!"

Herbie was nose to nose with Raymond now. "You're not Mr. Baseball. You're Mr. Slime-ball!"

Ray tried to smile. "Say, Herbie, ever hear the one about the two cannon balls that got married?"

"Yeah, they had a little BB. You tell the same dumb joke over and over. Don't try to change the subject."

"You're hurting my nose," Ray said softly.

Herbie backed off and looked away. "You know how disappointed my uncle is going to be? How could you say we're baseball greats?"

Raymond ran for the door. "I've got just the thing," he said, holding up a finger. "Don't move."

Ray dashed home on his bike.

When he returned, five minutes later, Herbie was still sitting on the bed.

"This is what we need," Ray said as he flipped Herbie a baseball cap.

Herbie looked at it. The cap was bright gold with the words, "Laurel Beef" in black.

"Where did you get this?"

"My dad wore 'em when he played city ball last year."

"I'm not wearing this, Ray."

"Sure you are! The kids down at the park don't know us. They'll be from different schools. When they see us in these caps, they'll think we're big shots."

Herbie watched Ray put his cap on. It fell down to his eyebrows.

"Just have to fix that thingy in the back," Ray said as he moved his over to the last notch.

"There," Ray replied as he put it back on. "Now we're baseball greats. Let's go!"

Herbie shook his head. He didn't feel like any baseball great and he didn't feel like joining any team.

Slowly, he adjusted his baseball cap, and picked up the glove off the kitchen table. Herbie wished things were as easy as Ray made them seem.

Reluctantly, he followed Ray outside to their bikes.

The First Practice

As the boys parked their bikes and walked across the green, they saw a bunch of kids around Uncle Dwight.

"Look what a big shot your uncle is," Ray said. "He's carrying a clipboard and has a whistle around his neck."

Herbie stopped cold when he recognized some of the kids. "That's John Greenweed, Phillip McDoogle, Margie Sherman, and Annabelle Louisa Hodgekiss! All the kids from school are on the team, Ray! I'm gettin' out of here," Herbie said as he ran for his bike.

"HEY BOYS! OVER HERE!" Uncle Dwight yelled.

Herbie stopped. His uncle had seen him. It was too late.

Slowly, Herbie walked across the green.

"Oh no!" Phillip McDoogle complained. "Not

those two. We'll *never* win a game!"

"They're instant outs at school," Annabelle Louisa Hodgekiss said, standing with her arms crossed.

Uncle Dwight raised his eyebrows. "Okay, kids, gather around. I want you to meet two more members of our team."

Everyone was pin quiet as Ray and Herbie joined them.

"This is Ray Martin, otherwise known as Mr. Baseball."

"Mr. Baseball?" everyone repeated.

"And this . . ." Uncle Dwight continued, "is my nephew Herbie."

"Your nephew?" Everyone looked shocked. No one said a word.

Finally Annabelle broke the silence. "My dad thought you two might be related. I just . . . didn't believe him."

Herbie took off his cap and fiddled with it.

Annabelle smiled. "I like your hats, boys. Gold is my favorite color."

Ray whispered to Herbie, "How come *she's* so friendly?"

Herbie knew why.

His uncle was the coach.

Uncle Dwight blew the whistle. "Okay, kids, let's start practice. The first thing we have to do is very important."

"You would know, Coach Jones," Annabelle interrupted. "My dad read about you in the newspaper. You're one of the best baseball players in the state."

Uncle Dwight smiled.

"What's the first thing?" John Greenweed asked. He wanted to play a game.

"We have to sing."

"Sing?" Everyone replied.

Herbie looked at Ray and raised his eyebrows. His uncle could be different sometimes.

"Sure. At your age, baseball should be fun. I want to make sure we start each practice on a good note. So, before we do anything else, I'm going to lead you in a very important song." And then Uncle Dwight hummed, "Hmmmmmmm."

Most of the team had their mouths open as they watched Herbie's uncle sing and wave his arms in the air:

"Take me out to the ballgame,
Take me out with the crowd.
Buy me some peanuts and Cracker Jack!
I don't care if I never get back.

Oh, it's root, root, root for the hometeam,
If they don't win it's a shame.
For it's one, two, three strikes you're out
At the old ballgame!"

Everyone tried to sing along with Uncle Dwight the second time around.

"Now," he said, "we have an important second thing to do."

"Is it as much fun as the first?" Margie Sherman asked.

"Wait and see," Uncle Dwight said as he brought out a big brown bag.

"Refreshments!" Ray shouted.

"Help yourself to some roasted peanuts while I talk to you about baseball," Uncle Dwight replied.

All the kids cheered and clapped.

"He sure knows what's important," Ray said as he reached into the sack with two hands.

Coach Jones brought out a small blackboard. "These are the positions on a baseball team. Notice

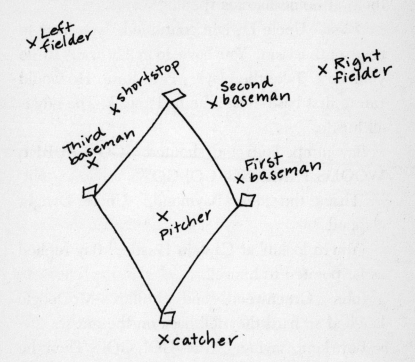

x
Center
fielder

x Left
fielder

x shortstop

Second
x baseman

x Right
fielder

Third
baseman
x

First
x baseman

x
pitcher

x catcher

people who play a base do NOT stand on it."

Everyone gathered around the diagram while they chomped on peanuts.

"There are three things you have to remember most in baseball," Uncle Dwight said as he held up three fingers.

Herbie took out his notepad from his back pocket. The first section was all poems. Herbie wrote a new heading: How to Be a Baseball Great. He wanted to take notes. Maybe he could study them at home like his spelling words.

"First," Uncle Dwight continued, "you have to have enthusiasm. You have to really want to do your best. Take the player, Pete Rose. He would run to first base even if he had a walk. The guy is all hustle."

Ray jumped up and shouted, "GO LAUREL WOODS PARK! GO! GO! GO!"

"That's the idea, Raymond," Uncle Dwight clapped.

"You're lookin' at Captain Hustle," Ray replied as he pointed to himself.

John Greenweed and Phillip McDoogle laughed so hard they fell back on the grass.

Ray kept saying, "GO! GO! GO!" Then he leaned over and whispered to Herbie, "This baseball business is gonna be a cinch!"

Herbie wasn't so sure.

He wrote down the words,

1. Enthoosiasum like Pete Rose.

"Okay, kids," Uncle Dwight continued. "You know we have one hour of practice each morning at the park. Well, the real practice is what *you* do on your own. Find someone to play catch with. Practice your throwing."

Herbie wrote down the second important thing about baseball.

2. Pracktise on your one.

Then he jabbed Raymond. "We have to play catch this afternoon."

"But, I don't have a mitt yet," Ray replied.

"There's one in our attic," Herbie said.

Ray made a face. Herbie knew why. Ray never liked to practice anything.

"The third thing I want to tell you is, Don't give up!"

Herbie wrote the three important words down on his notepad.

3. Don't give up!

Then he underlined them.

When he finished that, he copied down the diagram from the blackboard.

"Okay, let's have some batting practice!"

All the kids lined up at home plate.

Behind Annabelle.

"Hey, I need some people outfield to shag balls," Uncle Dwight said.

Herbie was glad to lose his place in line. "I'll help," he said.

Several players joined Herbie in the outfield.

Annabelle took out her batting gloves and smoothed them over her fingers. She did a few knee bends and breathing exercises.

"Come on," Phillip complained, "I want my turn."

Annabelle paid no attention to Phillip. She tapped the dirt off her cleats with the bat and then took a wide stance. She even checked to see if her knuckles were lined up.

"You've been well coached," Uncle Dwight remarked.

Annabelle beamed. "My dad worked with me."

BLAM!

WHAM!

CRACK!

Annabelle hit every ball Uncle Dwight pitched across the plate. Even the high ones and the low ones.

"You're a great contact hitter, Annabelle," Uncle Dwight said. "You'll be our leadoff batter." Annabelle held her head high as she ran to first base.

When it came time for Ray's turn, everybody in the field lay down. John Greenweed used second base for a pillow and pretended to snore, "Han shoo . . . Han shoo . . . Han shoo . . ."

Uncle Dwight turned around and snapped, "This is not naptime! Get up and play ball!"

Ray hit the first pitch. It was a nubber and it rolled three feet.

Uncle Dwight looked at Ray's stance. "You need to get your feet more even, and put your right elbow away from your body. Don't take anymore golf swings. Swing level like this."

Ray watched his coach.

"Okay," Uncle Dwight said as he walked back to the mound. "Hit this one right."

Ray took a level swing.

CRACK! The ball shot right by third base.

"That's the way, Raymond. Keep working on it. You're a hitter, Captain Hustle!"

Raymond made a toothy smile. "YAHOO! LAUREL WOODS PARK!" he shouted. Then he handed the bat to Herbie. "I'm a hitter, did you hear?"

Herbie took the bat. Now he felt worse. His buddy wasn't a loser. Just him.

Herbie tried to remember how to hold the bat.

Uncle Dwight pitched the ball.

WHIFF! Herbie missed.

WHIFF! WHIFF! Herbie missed three times.

Uncle Dwight ran over and checked Herbie's batting stance. "Hold your bat back more, Herbie. Get that left elbow up. Watch the ball."

Coach Jones pitched the ball again.

WHIFF!

Phillip McDoogle looked at John Greenweed at second base. "We've got a real Captain Whiff at the plate," he whispered.

As the boys laughed, Herbie felt his throat getting dry and raspy.

When his uncle pitched the next ball, he could barely see it. Herbie's eyes were filling with tears.

"We can work on your hitting tomorrow, Slugger," Uncle Dwight said. "Okay, kids, practice is over."

Phillip took John and Annabelle aside. "Everyone can hit on this team but Herbie. And he's the coach's nephew."

They shook their heads as they walked off the field.

Herbie didn't know what they said, but he knew it was about him.

I'll show them, he thought as he wiped a tear with his sleeve. He threw his mitt in his basket and stormed home on his bike.

Raymond tore after him.

5

The Monster Ball

"HURRY UP!" Herbie called from the top of the attic stairs.

Raymond trudged up each step. "What's the rush?"

"I've got to get you a mitt so we can practice."

Ray looked at his buddy and grinned. "I told you these "Laurel Beef" hats would make a difference. Once I got mine on right, I became a baseball great. I'm a hitter!"

"Yeah, well this hat doesn't work for me." Herbie picked up a mitt from a box of old stuff and threw it at Ray.

Ray caught it. Then he looked across the attic floor. "Hey, is that your uncle's room?"

"Yeah, why?"

"I've never seen it."

"It's just a room. Let's go practice."

Ray ran across the attic. "Come on, Double 0 3 0! It's time to spy!"

Herbie pointed to his buddy. "Only if you help me with baseball afterwards."

"Promise," Ray said as he ducked into the little room. "Wow! What a mess!"

Herbie nodded. "Mom never touches it. Uncle Dwight likes it this way—messy."

Ray walked over and looked at the trophies on the bookshelf. "Look at all this gold and silver!"

Herbie took one off the shelf and polished it with his T-shirt. "My uncle played three sports. He was a football, basketball, and baseball great."

Ray looked at the cartons of books and record albums. "Where are those bags he brought?"

"They would be hard to find in this mess."

And then Ray looked under the bed. "Help! What's that?"

Herbie got down and looked. "That's just the Monster Ball." Herbie rolled it out.

"Oh yeah," Ray replied, "you were going to tell me about the Mo . . . mo . . . monster ball."

"It's a basketball really. But don't tell my uncle that. He drew a monster face on it a long time ago with permanent black felt marker. He says the

Monster Ball knows everything. Sometimes when I have a problem, he asks the Monster Ball to help me."

Ray looked interested. "What does the Monster Ball say?"

"Lots of things, but only Uncle Dwight can hear his voice. He tells me what the Monster Ball says."

Ray looked at the funny face on the basketball and laughed. "Your uncle is a weirdo."

Herbie agreed. "I've known that for some time now. But, he's fun. It's like having an older brother."

Ray looked under the bed again. "Here it is!" he shouted. And he pulled out a duffle bag.

"Look," Ray said in a sneaky voice. "It's even unzipped."

"Put it back," Herbie replied. "I'm not going through my uncle's stuff."

Ray gave Herbie a look. "A deal's a deal."

"But that's being nosey," Herbie objected.

"So, spies are supposed to be nosey. Don't you watch TV? They always go through the guy's suitcase."

Herbie shook his head. "Okay, *you* take a look."

Ray poked his nose in the bag.

"Aaaauuugh!" Ray groaned. "What's that awful smell?" Ray pulled out a handful of socks. They were brown around the heels and toes.

Herbie started to laugh. "Serves you right. That's Uncle Dwight's laundry. He always brings it home from college."

"Gee," Ray said. "The guy can't throw clothes into a washing machine? Even *I* can do that."

Just as Ray put the socks back, he saw an index card. "Hey, it's got a drawing on it. Look!"

Herbie was curious. He took a quick peek. "It's a happy face with eyelashes and . . . earrings!"

"Eeyew!" Ray replied, "Earrings! But I can't read it. It's in cursive."

Herbie grabbed the index card from Ray. He wanted to end the spying business and get on with practice. Herbie read the card aloud:

Dwight,
    Wedding, Center Church
      July 13th 4:00 p.m.
Wear suit. Pick up ring
at Gem's Jewelers.

                                  C.

Ray dropped down to the bed. "Wow! Your uncle is going to be a broom."

"Not a broom, dummy, a groom. And we don't know that he's getting married. He's just picking up a wedding ring for someone who wears earrings . . . and who's name begins with a C."

Ray moved his eyebrows up and down. "Hmmm . . . Interesting," he mumbled. "I wonder who the C lady is . . ."

"*Ray*," Herbie said, "my uncle would have told us if he was getting married."

"He didn't tell you he was coming this summer."

"Yeah," Herbie replied, "but getting married is a *biggie*. He would have told us that."

As Herbie put the index card back in the bag and pushed it back under the bed, he thought about the idea of his uncle getting married. He half liked the idea. If his uncle was going on a honeymoon, Herbie wouldn't have to play ball.

"Come on Ray, let's get out of here."

Ray walked out of the attic room and picked up the mitt he had left on the floor. When he read the name penned on the side, he dropped it cold.

"What are you doing?"

"That mitt belongs to your sister. HER name is written on it."

"So? She played baseball in a pigtail league."

"Well, I'm not usin' a girl's mitt. NO WAY!" And Ray stomped across the attic floor.

"RAYMOND MARTIN, YOU PROMISED!" Herbie yelled after him.

Ray turned at the top of the stairs. "I promised to help you become a baseball great, but NOT with that thing. See you tomorrow."

Herbie threw down his own mitt. Now who could he practice with?

He looked at the two mitts on the attic floor.

Olivia?

6

Olivia

Herbie found his sister in the kitchen doing the sticky pancake dishes. She had just gotten started.

She was NOT in a good mood.

It sounded like she was breaking the dishes, not washing them.

Herbie tapped her on the shoulder, "Hi, Olivia," he said. He was *very* careful not to call her by the nickname he had for her—Olive.

"WHAT DO YOU WANT, ERB?" she snapped loudly.

Herbie knew this wouldn't be easy. He decided to make it as pleasant as possible. "I'll do those dishes for you."

Olivia turned around. The soap on her hands dripped onto the floor. "You will?" And then after she paused, she added, "Why?" She knew when her brother wanted something.

"I need you to play catch with me for awhile."

Herbie held up her mitt. "You know, base-ball."

Olivia took off her apron and laid it on the table. "Anything is better than doing dishes. Besides, I enjoy playing ball. You've got a deal!"

Herbie followed his sister out to the backyard. She was a full head taller than he was. He noticed she had her long hair pulled back in a plaid shoe-lace.

Olivia threw the ball to Herbie right away.

He dropped it.

Olivia tried not to laugh. "Herbie, you have the mitt on the wrong hand. Put your mitt on your left hand. Throw with your right."

Herbie switched hands. Then he threw his sister the ball. It went to the left and rolled into the petunias.

Olivia picked up the ball and then dropped to the grass on her knees. "Get down like me."

"Huh?"

"For working on our throwing and catching. My

pigtail coach said if you kneel, you work your arm muscles more."

Herbie kneeled on the grass.

"Now, when I throw you the ball, squeeze your mitt."

Herbie waited for Olivia to throw the ball to him.

She did.

PLOP!

It hit his mitt and then bounced out again.

"Do you think I'm a loser, Olive?" Herbie asked.

Olivia decided not to act bugged that he used her nickname. "No, Erb. Nobody in our family is. You just haven't had any baseball experience. It takes time. Listen, squeeze your mitt when the ball is in it. Then be sure to put the other hand over it. Don't let that ball pop out."

Herbie tossed his sister the ball.

She reached high in the air and caught it. Wow, Herbie thought, she was good. Then she threw him another ball.

PLOP!

Herbie squeezed his mitt. "I GOT IT!" he shouted. Boy, that felt good! he thought.

"Now, when you throw," Olivia continued, "bring your arm all the way back like this and then follow through."

Herbie watched his sister pantomime a good throw.

He copied her.

Olivia reached to the right and caught it. "Better. It just takes practice."

Practice.

Herbie remembered writing the word in his notepad. That's what was going to make Herbie a baseball great. He knew it. He just had to keep practicing over and over and over.

After thirty minutes, Olivia stood up and smiled. "Good, Herbie. Now I'll show you where the apron is."

Herbie frowned. He hated doing dishes. But a deal was a deal. And he was not going to fink out of it like ol' Raymond Martin.

While Herbie scrubbed the syrup off the plates with a Brillo pad, Olivia hopped on her bike and rode off.

Fifteen minutes later, Herbie was still washing dishes. His dad came in the kitchen with the mail and yawned. He turned the stove on to heat the kettle of water. "Thought you were practicing baseball today, Herbie," he said.

"I did."

"Hmmm," Mr. Jones set the mail down on the table and took an apple out of the fruit bowl. "I can remember catching fly balls in center field," and he tossed the apple high in the air.

Herbie turned around and watched his dad catch it. He squeezed his hands just like Olivia told Herbie to do.

"Want to toss me an apple, Dad?" Herbie asked.

Mr. Jones threw Herbie the apple.

It slipped right through Herbie's soapy hands and splashed in the dish water.

"Hey! You're getting yourself all wet. Dry your hands. Let's play some serious fruit ball here, son." Mr. Jones selected an orange from the bowl this time. "Now, get ready! You weren't ready before."

Mr. Jones threw the orange to Herbie. Herbie caught it with both hands and then returned it. "Want to see how many times we can toss it back and forth, Dad?"

"Let's work on a world's record," he said.

"One," Herbie counted.

"Two," Mr. Jones replied. Both of them kept tossing the orange back and forth.

Just when Mr. Jones said eight, the kettle whistled. "Never mind, Herbie, just concentrate. If you concentrate, you can do anything."

"Nine," Herbie replied, ignoring the shrill of the kettle.

By the time they got to thirty, the kettle was hopping on the stove.

Mr. Jones laughed. "Well, guess we'll have to continue our record another time," he said as he turned off the flame.

Herbie flipped the orange back into the bowl, and then finished the dishes.

That night after dinner, Herbie went outside to the backyard by himself. His dad had left for work. Uncle Dwight was asleep on the couch. Olivia was baby-sitting, and Mrs. Jones was relaxing in the bathtub with a book.

Herbie noticed his mom had hung out his uncle's sheets. Perfect, he thought.

He got the baseball, kneeled in the grass and threw the ball at the sheet.

Each time he practiced throwing, he brought his arm way back and followed through like his sister told him. Then he got up and picked up the ball and did the same thing over.

Herbie kept throwing at the sheet till the moon came out.

And then he threw some more.

7

Sleigh Bells

"I HAVE TO LEAVE IN FIVE MINUTES. IF YOU WANT AN EGG YOU BETTER GET DOWN HERE NOW!" Mrs. Jones was calling for the second time up the attic stairs.

Herbie looked at his mom. She had her purple-striped waitress uniform on. It was Thursday which was the beginning of her work week at Dipping Donuts.

"Your uncle can be impossible at times," she said tapping her foot.

Herbie picked up a grape off the kitchen table and tried to hit it with his spoon. He was getting worried. What if he struck out again at practice? He hadn't worked on his hitting.

"DWIGHT JONES!" she hollered again.

Olivia peeked her head around the kitchen corner. Mr. Jones did, too. "Hey, I have to get some shut eye," he complained.

"Well, *I* have to go to work," Mrs. Jones replied. "Here's the spatula. You can get your brother's breakfast."

Mrs. Jones dashed out the door and drove off in their family station wagon to work.

Mr. Jones looked at the spatula and yawned.

Just then the attic door flew open. "What time is it?" Uncle Dwight asked, as he ran all ten fingers through his uncombed hair.

"Nine," Herbie said looking at the kitchen clock.

"NINE! I'm supposed to be at work now!"

"You better take Olivia's bike and eat something on the way," Mr. Jones said. "I was going to cook you something. Got a hot griddle here."

Dwight reached in his shirt pocket and pulled out two Twinkies. "How 'bout frying these up?" he said peeling back the cellophane.

Herbie dropped his spoon. "Man, fried Twinkies. Neato!"

Mr. Jones grumbled something as he turned the Twinkies over a few times on the grill.

"Flip it to me, brother!" Dwight called.

Mr. Jones shook his head as he flipped the fried Twinkies. Dwight caught one in each hand. Then he raced outside to the garage. His shirt was untucked and his hair still uncombed. Herbie watched him from the back porch. He saw him run along the driveway with Olivia's bike, jump onto the seat and ride off. All the while, the Twinkies were clenched between his teeth like two big cigars.

What a neat guy, Herbie thought.

When his uncle rounded the corner, Herbie went back to the table and continued hitting grapes.

BLAM!

He got off a real good one. Herbie watched it travel across the kitchen and then bounce off his dad's head.

"Herbie!" Mr. Jones growled. "I'm tired. I'm going to bed. Stop foolin' around!"

Fortunately, Herbie had an excuse to leave the kitchen. The doorbell rang.

It was Raymond.

Herbie *wasn't* glad to see him. He grabbed his mitt and headed out the door.

"I know you're probably mad," Ray said following Herbie down the steps, "but listen. I spent all afternoon and evening going through my baseball card collection. I told you I'd help you and I can." Ray reached into his back pocket. "I know what makes a baseball great. I have the formula."

No doubt it was another one of Ray's dumb ideas, Herbie thought, but he was mildly curious. "What formula?"

"Look what I have here in my hand."

"Baseball cards," Herbie replied.

"Yes, and look who's on them! The greatest ballplayers."

"So?"

"So, look at their names. All the greats have one sleigh bell names."

"Sleigh bells?"

"You know. Sounds. The word car has one sleigh bell. Baseball has two sleigh bells. We learned that in school a long time ago."

"You mean syllables?"

"Yeah, that's what they are! Listen to these greats with one sleigh bell names."

Herbie leaned forward. He couldn't be mad at

Ray any more. He was trying to help him with baseball.

Ray read off the list of greats:

Babe Ruth
Ty Cobb
Moose Haas
Fred Lynn
Jim Rice
Ron Cey
George Brett
Mike Schmidt
Stu Kemp
Mel Ott
Cy Young
Pete Rose
Wade Boggs
Ray Knight
Oil Can Boyd

Herbie scratched his head. "That's true. They're the REAL greats and they have one-syllable names."

"And look at your uncle—Dwight Jones! He's a

baseball great, too! Sure, it's true. That's why you and me are changing our names for the summer."

"We are?"

"You're Herb Jones—the baseball great!"

"Herb Jones? Herb Jones." Herbie kept repeating it. He liked the sound of his new name. "What about you—Raymond Martin?"

"You're lookin' at another baseball great—Ray Mart!"

"Ray Mart? That sounds like K-Mart."

"Don't knock it, Herb, we're baseball greats now!"

8

The Worst Sandwich

Herbie didn't feel like going to baseball practice, even with his new one-syllable name. "Want to take the long way by the swimming hole?" he asked Ray.

"Sure, Herb Jones. Let's go!"

The boys rode their bikes along the river as Ray's dog, Shadow, followed closely behind.

Suddenly, Herbie stopped. "Did you hear that?"

"What?" Ray screetched his brakes.

"There's splashing coming from the swimming hole! Who would be swimming at 9:15 in the morning?" Herbie parked his bike and went to check it out.

"This looks like an interesting spy mission, Double 0 3 0," Raymond said, as he parked his bike next to Herbie's.

As the boys peeked over the bushes, they could see someone swimming in the middle of the river. "It's a lady and she's wearing a bathing cap," Ray whispered.

Herbie looked at his buddy. "I'm not going to practice. I need to work on my hitting some more. If I go today, I'll just disappoint my uncle."

"Hey," Ray replied. "We're baseball greats now. We can miss a practice or two." Then he looked over at Shadow. He was on the lady's blanket sniffing her shoes, her towel, and then her brown-bag lunch.

"Come back here, Shadow!" Ray whispered.

"Look," Herbie pointed, "he's taking that lady's bag and bringing it to us."

Ray kneeled down on the grass. "Over here, boy. Give it to me."

Shadow dropped the bag and then nosed inside. A moment later he pulled out a sandwich.

"He's gonna eat it, Ray!" Herbie said.

Both boys dived on the dog, but it was too late. Shadow gulped the last bite.

"Great! Just great! Now what do we do?" Ray threw up his hands.

"We have to replace the sandwich. What kind was it?"

Ray gave Herbie a blank look. "You're askin' me? I didn't eat it—he did!" And he pointed to Shadow.

Herbie picked up the dog and opened his mouth. "I can tell by his breath." Herbie stuck his nose in Shadow's mouth. "Aaauuuugh!" Herbie said as he fell to the ground.

"What kind was it? Salami?" Ray asked.

"Worse than that," Herbie groaned.

"Egg?"

Herbie sat up and looked sick. "It was liver-wurst."

"That IS the worst sandwich," Ray agreed.

"Where can we get liverwurst fast?"

Ray thought for a minute. "Hey, my dad loves the stuff. I bet I have some in my fridge. I could put some on two slices of bread, pop it into a brown bag and be back here in five minutes."

"You're amazing, Ray Mart," Herbie said. "Get going. I'll guard the fort here."

Herbie watched Ray hop on his bike and speed off. Shadow barked behind him. Herbie knew

Ray's refrigerator was different. Finding liverwurst in it would be easy. Also artichoke hearts, but they didn't need any of those.

Herbie went back to the bushes. He could spy from there without being seen.

He watched the lady pull herself up onto the big rock and then turn toward the deeper part of the swimming hole. She gave herself a little push and then made a perfect dive into the river. She reminded Herbie of the movie star that swam in late movies on TV, Esther Williams.

Herbie thought the morning was turning out to be fun.

After five minutes, the lady started to get out of the water. Herbie began to get nervous. What if she noticed her lunch was gone before Ray returned?

As the lady waded back up the shore, she took off her bathing cap.

Herbie took a step back. He knew that lady! It was Miss Pinkham—his teacher from third grade!

Herbie stared at her bathing suit. It was red with yellow butterflies. The butterflies had purple antennas.

Herbie looked away. It didn't seem right that he

should see his TEACHER in a swimsuit. Where was Ray?

Herbie looked back at his teacher. She was lying on the blanket with her eyes closed.

Herbie breathed a little easier.

Ten minutes later he heard someone pedaling up the pathway. It was Ray and he had a brown bag with him. Herbie quickly motioned for him to be quiet and to come over by the bushes.

"Look who that lady is!" Herbie whispered.

Ray looked over the bushes. "I know her?"

"Of course you do—that's Miss Pinkham!"

"MISS PINKHAM?"

Herbie covered Ray's mouth. "Shhhh!"

"Oh boy, and we didn't have liverwurst in our refrigerator."

"So what did you make?"

"I made her a liver sandwich."

"A LIVER SANDWICH?"

"Shhhh!" Ray whispered. "She's still sleeping. I looked in the meat crisper, and lucky for me, there was some liver. She won't know the difference."

"Well, let's get this lunch bag back on her blanket and cut out of here," Herbie replied.

The two boys tiptoed across the sandy riverbank. Miss Pinkham still had her eyes closed and she was snoring softly.

As they got closer, they dropped the lunch on the blanket and then took off.

Just before they got to the bushes, Shadow came flying overhead landing on both of the boys. Herbie and Ray fell backwards as Shadow licked their faces and barked loudly.

As soon as the boys pushed Shadow away, they turned to look at their teacher. One eye popped open. Immediately she sat up. "Boys! What a surprise!"

Herbie stuttered, "We . . . we . . . we were in the neighborhood so we thought we would stop by and say hello."

Ray looked at Herbie and whispered, "You sound like my mother."

Herbie gave Ray a quick jab to the side.

"Yeah," Ray joined in. "Here we are in the same neighborhood."

"Sit down boys," Miss Pinkham said.

Herbie felt uneasy. He was right next to the butterflies with the purple antennas.

"I just love a good morning swim. I have the river to myself."

"Just you and the tadpoles," Ray grinned.

Miss Pinkham cringed. Then she quickly changed the subject. "So what have you boys been doing this summer?"

"Well," Ray replied, "we've been spending lots of time in the library. We just love those psycho pedias."

Herbie looked away. Ray was overdoing it again.

"Great!" Miss Pinkham said half laughing. "I got my class assignment in the mail this week. I'm teaching fourth grade this fall."

Herbie turned around. "You are? I hope I have you." And then his face turned red.

"You do." Miss Pinkham smiled.

Ray jumped up, crossed his fingers, his legs, and closed his eyes tightly. "Tell me I'm in your room too. Please?"

"You are."

Ray leaped in the air and yodeled, "YAHOO!" When he came back down, he slapped his buddy five. "This is gonna be our best year yet! Ol' Herb Jones and Ray Mart are gonna be in the same class again!"

Miss Pinkham reached for her lunch bag. "You

boys want part of my sandwich? I always get hungry after a swim."

Suddenly the boys stood up like soldiers.

"We have to go now," Herbie said as he grabbed Ray's arm. "Right Ray?"

"Right, Herb."

As the boys walked backwards, they bumped into each other.

"Well, I'll probably see you boys at the park sometime. I play tennis a lot." Miss Pinkham waved good-bye.

Just as the boys got to their bikes, they heard a shrill scream.

Herbie looked at Ray. "That liver you put in her sandwich . . ."

"Yeah?"

"It was cooked wasn't it?"

"I didn't have time. I just slid it right onto the bread, blood and all."

"HOW COULD YOU!" Herbie yelled as he hopped on his bike and pedaled away.

"WAIT FOR ME!" Ray called after him.

9

A Talk with
the Monster Ball

That night before Uncle Dwight came home, Herbie laid on his bed writing. His door was ajar.

Olivia came by and peeked her head in Herbie's room. She had on a purple two-piece bathing suit.

"You should have been down at the swimming hole, Erb. The water was great!"

Herbie looked up from his notebook. "I was."

"You were? I didn't see you. I was there since noon."

"I was there this morning."

Olivia took a step into her brother's room. "You cut baseball practice?"

Herbie nodded. "I gotta work some more on my hitting before I show up again."

Olivia's eyes widened. "ERB JONES, YOU are in big trouble!"

Herbie sat up. "I am?"

"When you're on a team, you NEVER miss a practice."

"N-n-never?"

Olivia shook her head. "Not unless you're real sick. Uncle Dwight is going to be so mad!"

Herbie watched his sister turn and leave the room. Quickly, he got up and closed the door. Then he put a chair in front of it.

Ten minutes later, there was a knock on Herbie's door. "Herbie? You in there?" It was Uncle Dwight.

Herbie managed to get a word out, "S . . . sure, come in. The door's not locked."

Uncle Dwight turned the doorknob. The door didn't open. Finally he gave it a push and knocked the chair over.

"Hey, Herbie," Uncle Dwight said, stepping over the chair.

Herbie swallowed hard.

He wondered if his uncle was going to be *real*

mad that he didn't go to practice.

"What's up, Herbie?"

"Nothing much."

"You writing some poems?"

Herbie nodded.

"That's great. Want to bring them up and read a few to the Monster Ball and me?"

Herbie looked at his uncle. He was wearing an old sweatshirt with the letters "UCONN" on it. He had a baseball cap on and his sneakers had holes in them. His shirt was still untucked under his sweatshirt.

"Come on, let's go," Uncle Dwight nudged Herbie.

Herbie slowly followed his uncle up the attic stairs to his room. The sun was still pouring through the open windows. It made crazy looking shadows on the attic floor, Herbie thought.

Herbie sat down on the unmade bed. Uncle Dwight reached under the bed and put the Monster Ball on a chair. "We want to hear your poems," he said.

Herbie opened his notebook and read one.

I like spiders
And the way they crawl.
You can find them in dark places.
But not at the mall.

Uncle Dwight held the Monster Ball up to his right ear. "He likes your poem. Do you have another one?"

Herbie flipped a page in his notebook and read his latest.

The lady can dive and
Swim real far.
She looks like Ester Williams,
The movie star.

Uncle Dwight raised his eyebrows up and down. Then he moved the Monster Ball to his left ear. "He really likes that poem! Now, he wants to know why you didn't show up at practice today."

Herbie closed his notepad. He didn't feel like talking.

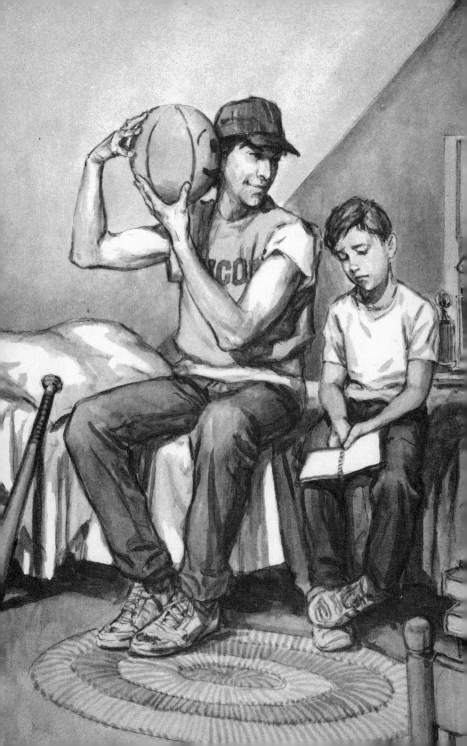

Uncle Dwight held the Monster Ball up to his ear again. "Hmmm, I see."

"What did he say?" Herbie couldn't help wondering.

"He said you didn't want to go to practice because you thought you would just strike out again."

"How did he know?"

"The Monster Ball knows all," Uncle Dwight replied.

Herbie didn't want to look at his uncle. He felt rotten about his hitting. And now, he felt rotten about cutting practice.

Herbie looked down at the attic floor. "I bet you're real disappointed in me."

"Not at all. In fact, I'm proud of you."

Herbie looked up. "You're proud of me?"

"You're trying to do something new. You're giving it a real effort. Look how well you do other things," he said as he tousled Herbie's hair. "You write poems, read books, you know how to be a friend. You're one great guy!"

"You don't think I stink as a baseball player?"

"No. You don't stink. You're learning. You're making progress. Yesterday you whiffed at every ball. Next time you'll get a piece. It's just a matter of time. But you have to come to practice. We're playing Beechwood on Saturday."

"Our first game . . ." Herbie gulped.

Uncle Dwight got up and walked over to his bookcase. "Don't worry about striking out, Herbie. Everyone does. Even great batters like the Mighty Casey. Ever hear of him?"

Herbie shook his head.

"You should. You're a poet. Listen to this," said Uncle Dwight, as he read the poem, "Casey at the Bat." When he got to the end, Herbie read over his shoulder.

> "And now the pitcher holds the ball, and now
>   he lets it go,
>   And now the air is shattered by the force
>   of Casey's blow.
>
> Oh, somewhere in this favored land the sun
>   is shining bright;
>   The band is playing somewhere, and
>   somewhere hearts are light,
> And somewhere men are laughing, and little
>   children shout;

But there is no joy in Mudville—mighty Casey has struck out."

"Casey was a great ballplayer and he whiffed?" Herbie looked shocked.

Uncle Dwight nodded.

Herbie took the book in his hands. "He must have felt bad when it happened."

Uncle Dwight nodded again.

"Can I copy this poem in my notebook?"

"Sure. As a matter of fact, I'm pooped. I just finished playing four games of volleyball with a group of senior citizens. I have to take a nap before dinner. Go write some more great poems, Herbie. Maybe even one about baseball. I'll pitch you a few after dinner."

"You will?"

Uncle Dwight yawned. "Sure, Herbie." And then he laid down on his bed with the Monster Ball and fell asleep.

Herbie watched his uncle snore for a few minutes. Then he took out his notebook and wrote two poems. He tore the page off and put it next to his uncle's pillow.

Cutting pracktise is a
Dumb thing to do.
We're gonna beat Beechwood
So don't be blue.

My coach is tall.
My coach is nice.
He helps me play ball
And he eats lots of rice.

It Happened in the Moonlight

After dinner, Uncle Dwight drove Herbie to Laurel Woods Park. They went to the far diamond where no one was playing.

Herbie liked the lights in the park.

He also liked the moon.

It reminded him of the night he worked on his throwing.

"HERB JONES!" a voice called from the other end of the park.

Herbie looked over. It was Ray Mart.

"I gotta talk to you about something. It's real important."

"After practice, Ray Mart."

"Want to shag a few balls, Ray?" Uncle Dwight asked. "You owe me a practice, too."

Ray reluctantly walked out to center field. He didn't look happy. Herbie wondered why.

"You have to remember," Uncle Dwight said from the mound. "It takes time, okay, Herbie?"

Uncle Dwight pitched the first ball.

WHIFF.

WHIFF. Herbie missed the next one, too.

But, he knicked the third ball.

"I GOT A PIECE!" Herbie shouted.

"YOU GOT A PIECE!" Uncle Dwight shouted.

"You got a piece!" said a third voice from the tennis courts.

It was Miss Pinkham.

Uncle Dwight swung around. "Clara Pinkham!"

"Dwight Jones!" Miss Pinkham called back.

Suddenly Miss Pinkham ran into Uncle Dwight's arms.

Herbie dropped his bat.

Raymond dropped his mitt.

Uncle Dwight was lifting their teacher and twirling her around twice!

"Okay," Uncle Dwight said as he put Miss Pinkham down. "Clara and I can get together after the practice."

Raymond and Herbie looked at each other. "Get together after practice?"

"Right now, it's business," Uncle Dwight continued. "Here comes your next pitch."

Herbie let the ball go by. "You *know* Miss Pinkham?" he asked Uncle Dwight.

"Of course I do. We grew up in the same neighborhood. Her brother and I were best friends."

Herbie was relieved. He ran after the ball and threw it back to his uncle.

For the next half hour, Uncle Dwight pitched ninety balls. Herbie missed forty-five of them. He got a piece of forty-three of them. He hit two into right field.

"WAY TO GO, HERBIE!" Miss Pinkham yelled.

Herbie smiled.

Raymond said nothing.

"Okay, Captain Hustle," Uncle Dwight said, "it's your turn."

"Nah, I have to get home."

Herbie handed his bat to his uncle. "You go on without me, Uncle Dwight. I'll hitch a ride with Ray. See you, Miss Pinkham."

As the boys rode down the street, Herbie asked Ray what was the matter.

"It's bad news," Ray said as he parked his bike in front of Herbie's house. "Look at this." Ray pulled a piece of paper out of his pocket and handed it to Herbie.

$$-3 \quad \text{☺} \quad \textit{Good Effort}$$

$$
\begin{array}{cccc}
\begin{array}{r} 6 \\ \times\, 3 \\ \hline 18 \end{array} &
\begin{array}{r} 4 \\ \times\, 4 \\ \hline 16 \end{array} &
\begin{array}{r} 8 \\ \times\, 3 \\ \hline 24 \end{array} &
\begin{array}{r} 6 \\ \times\, 9 \\ \hline 15 \checkmark \end{array}
\end{array}
$$

$$
\begin{array}{cccc}
\begin{array}{r} 5 \\ \times\, 4 \\ \hline 20 \end{array} &
\begin{array}{r} 7 \\ \times\, 7 \\ \hline 48 \checkmark \end{array} &
\begin{array}{r} 4 \\ \times\, 9 \\ \hline 36 \end{array} &
\begin{array}{r} 6 \\ \times\, 6 \\ \hline 12 \checkmark \end{array}
\end{array}
$$

"It's an old math paper of yours," Herbie said. "One of your better ones. You just missed three."

"Yeah, but do you see Miss Pinkham's happy face in the corner? It's just like the one we found in your uncle's duffle bag."

Herbie looked again. The happy face had eyelashes. "You don't think Miss Pinkham wrote that note to my uncle?"

"Well, I wasn't positive until . . . tonight," Raymond frowned, "but *now* I know *who* the C lady is for sure—Miss *Clara* Pinkham."

"MISS PINKHAM? Our teacher? You think *she's* the C lady? You're crazy, Ray Mart."

"Didn't you see the way they hugged at the park?"

"They're old friends."

"Friends don't hug like that. Miss Pinkham was airborne when he twirled her! And you were *there* when your uncle called her Clara."

"That's her first name, Ray."

"She's a teacher. You don't call teachers by their first name. Nobody does."

Herbie headed for the door. "Ray, you're blowing this whole thing up. What do you care anyway?"

"Don't you know what this means?" Ray asked.

Herbie shrugged. "If my uncle marries Miss Pinkham, I'll be related to my teacher."

"Wrong, Herbie. You'll be related to MY TEACHER. You won't be able to have Miss Pinkham for fourth grade. She'll be Mrs. Jones, your *aunt*. Everyone knows you can't have your aunt for your teacher."

Herbie looked at his buddy. "We wouldn't be in the same room next year?"

"Nope. You'd be in the OTHER fourth grade."

"But," Ray held up one finger, "we have one chance. When they are at the church on July thirteenth, you and me show up. When the minister says is there a reason why these two shouldn't be married, we speak up."

"Huh?"

"Haven't you seen that on TV? We tell the minister that we have to be in fourth grade together because we're best friends. He'll understand. No way he'll let them get married when he knows that."

Herbie laughed. "Ray! We don't even know they are getting married for sure."

"I will tomorrow."

"Tomorrow?"

Ray picked up his bike and hopped on. "Tomorrow I'm going to Miss Pinkham's house and ask her face to face. I'll get the facts for sure."

Herbie was impressed. "You know where she lives?"

"Hey, you're looking at the number one spy in Laurel Woods."

Ray's Toughest Spy Mission

Ray had a problem. He *didn't* know where Miss Pinkham lived.

The next morning as he sat on the front porch picking fleas off his dog, he thought about Annabelle.

She knew where Miss Pinkham lived. She had bragged about visiting her house one day in class when she had delivered some Girl Scout cookies.

Ray walked back inside. All he had to do was find his mom's red telephone book. That was usually difficult, but never impossible for a spy like Raymond.

This time he found it in the refrigerator.

Ray turned to the H section. Hodgekiss was written right next to House of Beauty and Happy Pizza.

Raymond dialed Annabelle's number.

She picked it up on the second ring. "Hodgekiss residence," she said politely.

Raymond hung up.

He realized he had never called a girl before. He wondered if he could.

Then he thought about fourth grade. He HAD to do it. He had to know if he and Herbie were going to be in the same class.

Ray redialed Annabelle's number. This time he held his nose. Calling a girl was worse than eating a liver sandwich, he thought.

Annabelle picked it up on the first ring, "Hodgekiss residence," she said.

Raymond managed a weak "Hello?"

"Is this the operator?" Annabelle asked.

Ray unplugged his nose. He was no operator. "Is . . . is this Isabelle Hogkiss?"

Annabelle was quiet for a moment. "WHO do you want?"

"Eh . . . Annabelle Kisshog?"

"If this is a joke, it is not very funny."

"This is Raymond Martin," Ray said finally.

It was quiet on the other end of the phone.

"Annabelle? You there?" Raymond asked.

"What do YOU want, Raymond Martin?"

Ray noticed there was an edge to her voice. "I need an address."

"Whose?"

"Miss Pinkham's."

"Our teacher, Miss Pinkham's?"

"Yeah."

"Why?"

"Because."

"Because why?"

"It's a top secret. Can't say," Ray replied.

"Well, I'm not giving it to you unless you tell me why you want it. How do I know you might not just ring her doorbell and run off?"

Ray was quiet. He wondered if Annabelle knew about the time he had done that to her house.

"No reason, no address," Annabelle said firmly.

"Okay, but can you keep a secret?" Ray asked.

"Of course I can."

Ray told Annabelle the whole story about how he and Herbie thought Miss Pinkham was getting married to Herbie's uncle and if that happened, they wouldn't be in the same class. Raymond thought Annabelle seemed very interested in the wedding part.

"So, you're going to knock on Miss Pinkham's door and ask her if she's getting married, just like that?"

"Yup."

"Raymond, that's not proper."

"What do you mean?"

"You don't just blurt something like that out. You have to work it in the conversation."

"Work it in the conversation?"

"It's the only polite thing to do. I think I can help."

"Why would you want to help?" Ray asked.

"Because if Miss Pinkham is getting married, I should know about it, too. After all, I am her best student. If I come along, I can work it in the conversation, about her getting married, and when I do, we'll find out."

Ray thought Annabelle made things complicated, but he needed the address and if Annabelle did go, she could show him how to get there. "Okay, meet you on the corner of Wainwright Crescent and Washington Avenue."

"Fine, just don't be late. And don't bring your dog."

Raymond wanted to end the conversation, so he didn't argue. "Good-bye," he said and hung up.

When he got to the corner, Annabelle was already there. She was holding a bouquet of flowers.

"What did you bring those for?" Ray asked, pointing to the flowers.

"You mean the roses?"

Raymond nodded as they walked along the sidewalk.

"I need them for the conversation."

"Are those roses gonna talk too?"

"No Raymond. These roses don't talk." Annabelle rolled her eyes. "Just leave things to me."

As they walked to Miss Pinkham's house, Raymond began to feel nervous. It was bad enough calling a girl let alone walking with one. He hoped no one would see them.

"Here it is," Annabelle said as they turned the corner. "Wind Tree Street. She lives in the third house. The yellow one."

Raymond looked at his teacher's house. The lawn was neatly trimmed, and there were tulips lining the pathway. In the picture window was a big ceramic owl sitting on a table.

"Now remember," Annabelle said as they walked up to Miss Pinkham's door, "let me do the talking."

Ray looked at Annabelle. She *always* had to be in charge, he thought.

Annabelle rang the doorbell once.

Raymond did too.

"You shouldn't have done that! It's rude to ring the doorbell twice."

Ray wrinkled his eyebrows. "You said to leave the talking to you. Not the doorbell ringing." And he rang the doorbell again.

Annabelle grabbed Ray's hand. "Stop that!"

When Miss Pinkham opened the door, she saw them standing there holding hands. "Well, hello! Won't you come in?"

Ray wanted to get away fast so he stepped right into the hallway. But Annabelle pulled him back by his T-shirt.

"We can't stay, Miss Pinkham, thank you. We just happened to be in the neighborhood so we thought we would drop by."

"Hmmmm," Miss Pinkham replied. "Seems

Raymond and I are bumping into each other a lot lately."

Raymond was glad now that Annabelle was doing the talking. He didn't want to talk about that morning at the river.

"So how have you been Miss Pinkham?" Annabelle asked politely.

"Fine, and you, Annabelle?"

"Fine. I brought you some roses from my garden."

"How lovely! Aren't you sweet. I love roses." Miss Pinkham smiled as she smelled one.

"Me too," Raymond said. He felt he should say one thing.

Annabelle glared at Raymond. "By the way, Miss Pinkham," Annabelle continued, "speaking of flowers always makes me think of weddings. You know, the bouquets that brides carry?"

"Mmmmm, yes," Raymond nodded.

Annabelle stepped on Ray's foot.

Miss Pinkham looked confused, but managed a smile. "That's true."

"And speaking of weddings, are you by chance in one the thirteenth of July?"

Miss Pinkham looked surprised.

Raymond leaned forward. Her answer was important.

"As a matter of fact, I am," Miss Pinkham replied.

"Oh," Annabelle sighed, "how wonderful! I just *love* weddings. Will you be wearing white lace?"

Ray pulled Annabelle's braid, "We have to go now, Miss Pinkham. See you later."

"Have a happy wedding!" Annabelle called from the sidewalk. And then when they turned the corner, she flared her nostrils at Raymond. "How dare you rush me like that. I don't even know what church she's getting married at."

"Center Church," Ray grumbled.

"Or what time," Annabelle continued.

"Four P.M."

Raymond stopped. "Is there anything *else* you want to know?"

"Well . . ." Annabelle said dreamily, "I'd love to know what kind of flowers will be in Miss Pinkham's wedding bouquet. Butterfly orchids? Lilies of the valley? White roses?"

Ray made a face. "I hope it's poison ivy."

"POISON IVY?" Annabelle stopped walking. "What a DREADFUL thing to say. Why, Miss

Pinkham would get a red rash all over her face, and when it came time . . ." Annabelle's voice got dreamy again, "to finalize their vows with a kiss, Herbie's uncle would get a red rash too."

"Eeyew," Ray groaned. "You had to go and say the K word. I gotta get out of here."

Ray ran home fast.

That night Ray made a quick phone call.

"Double 0 3 0?"

"Yeah, 9 9 2?"

"It's true. I was at Miss Pinkham's house and Miss Pinkham is marrying your uncle July thirteenth."

Herbie dropped the phone. When he picked it up, he said, "Ray, are you *sure*? I think I better check with my uncle about this."

"NO! DON'T DO THAT! If you do you'll blow the whole plan. We have to catch them by surprise."

"What plan?"

"Remember? You and me show up July thirteenth and tell the minister why they can't get married. It's foolproof! But, it's gotta be a top secret."

Herbie rested the receiver on his shoulder. Ray was desperate. If he didn't calm him down, he might blow the game against Beechwood on Saturday!

"Okay, Ray Mart. You have my word. We'll do it your way."

"Great!"

"But don't get your hopes up too high, 9 9 2."

Ray was quiet for a moment. Then he said, "Over and out, Double 0 3 0."

12

Knit Wits

"Where's Herbie?" Uncle Dwight asked Friday night as he got up from a nap on the couch. "I haven't seen him since dinner."

"He's outside throwing," Mrs. Jones replied.

"Throwing?" Uncle Dwight looked around. Who was Herbie playing catch with? Mr. Jones was watching the news on TV. Olivia was over at a friend's.

Uncle Dwight stepped out on the back porch.

Herbie was throwing a baseball at a towel on the clothesline. He watched Herbie bring his arm way back and then hurl the ball.

It missed the towel and landed smack inside Olivia's purple bathing suit. The top part!

Uncle Dwight put two thumbs up. Bull's-eye! he thought. Then he ducked back into the house.

He didn't think Herbie would want him to see.

Herbie covered his eyes as soon as he saw where the ball landed. Quickly he looked both ways before he went to get it.

When he turned around, Uncle Dwight could see the color of Herbie's face. Bright red!

"Can I borrow the car for an hour," Uncle Dwight asked Mrs. Jones.

"Sure, why?"

"I want to do something special with Herbie."

Mrs. Jones tossed him the keys and smiled.

Herbie got into the car reluctantly. "Where are we going? I need to practice more." And then he lowered his voice. "My aim is off a little."

Herbie had a real case of the butterflies.

"You'll see," Uncle Dwight said as he pulled out of the driveway.

"Herbie, we want to tell you something."

"We?" Herbie looked at the front seat. It was just his uncle and himself.

And then he looked in the backseat.

The Monster Ball was along for the ride. And he had his seatbelt on.

Herbie smiled.

"What makes this summer special," Uncle Dwight continued, "is being able to spend it with you. I'm really proud of your progress in baseball, Herbie. But most of all I just like being with you."

Herbie moved closer to his uncle. He wanted to say something nice but the words didn't come. He decided he would leave him another poem on his pillow tonight.

Herbie watched as his uncle pulled into the drive through of Burger Paradise.

"We're going here? We just had dinner."

"Do you have room for apple pie?"

Herbie grinned.

Uncle Dwight rolled the window down and waited for the voice to ask what he wanted. Herbie watched.

"Welcome to Paradise. May I help you?"

"Three apple pies."

"Three?" Herbie asked. And then he turned around and looked at the Monster Ball. "He said he better not. He prefers a Paradise pickle. He's on a diet."

Uncle Dwight laughed, then he spoke into the speaker board. "Make that two apple pies and one Paradise pickle."

"Thank you," the voice responded. "We hope you enjoy your trip to Paradise."

After Uncle Dwight and Herbie got their food, they took it back to the house, and walked up to the attic. Herbie carried the bag, and Uncle Dwight carried the Monster Ball.

"I want to share something with you, Herbie, that has helped me a lot before games."

Herbie set the apple pies on the table in his uncle's room. "You going to teach me how to play poker?"

Dwight shook his head. He reached into his duffle bag and pulled out a long multi-colored scarf. "I knit before games," he said.

Herbie didn't say anything.

Dwight held up the scarf. "Each night before a big game, I knit a few rows. See how long it's gotten in three years?"

Herbie looked at it. "Grandmother knits. But you don't look like a grandmother."

"I'm not. I knit because it relaxes me. There's a group of us guys that knit at the university. We call ourselves the Knit Wits."

Herbie cracked up. "I like that! So you're a Knit Wit?"

"One of the best." Then Uncle Dwight handed him two needles. One already had loops on it.

"Here, you try."

Herbie rolled his eyeballs. "I don't know about this."

"Try it." Uncle Dwight demonstrated. "Just take the needles and pull the tip into the loop, and then throw some yarn over it. It's easy."

Herbie took the needles and did what his uncle said.

"Hey! You've got it."

Herbie looked up at his uncle. "You won't tell Ray about this will you?"

"It's our secret. And the Knit Wits'."

After five minutes, Uncle Dwight reached for his apple pie. "Want to join me, Herbie?"

Herbie didn't hear him. He was concentrating too hard on his knitting.

Uncle Dwight smiled as he looked at Herbie. Then he took out the pickle and placed it next to the Monster Ball. He didn't like to eat alone.

13

The Big Game

It was noon on Saturday. The sun was directly overhead.

Uncle Dwight was sitting on the bench with his team. He was going over the lineup that was attached to his clipboard.

"Well, everyone's playing the whole six innings. Two kids are on vacation and one is sick. It's a good thing we have twelve players on our roster.

Phillip made a face. "That means Herbie has to bat at least three times. Boy, the air is gonna take a real beating today. Captain Whiff will be striking away."

Uncle Dwight shot a look at Phillip. "We're a team, Phillip. We support one another. If I hear any more bad remarks from you, you'll be on the bench and we'll play with eight!"

Annabelle flared her nostrils. "Coach Jones is

right. This is a team, and I bat first."

Uncle Dwight laughed.

"I am up first, right?" Annabelle asked in the next breath.

Uncle Dwight nodded. "You're batter number one."

Annabelle beamed.

Mrs. Jones was in the bleachers next to Mrs. Martin and in front of a big poster that had white and pink laurel flowers on it. Annabelle and Margie had painted them days ago.

Shadow was tied to the railing of the bleachers. He was sniffing a wrapper someone had dropped.

At the refreshment stand, Mr. Hodgekiss was wearing a flowered apron and stirring a big pot of chili that he had made himself.

Mrs. Hodgekiss was selling coffee, soda, and candy. A sign nailed to the booth said: ALL PROFITS GO TO THE LAUREL WOODS PARK PARENTS CLUB.

Mr. Jones was walking back and forth behind the backstop. He was restless and couldn't sit in the bleachers.

The umpire was sipping a cup of coffee.

The Beechwood Team was sitting on the opposite bench waiting for the umpire to finish his coffee and call out "PLAY BALL!"

Olivia bought a chili dog from Mr. Hodgekiss just about the time that the umpire threw his paper coffee cup into the litter can. "PLAY BALL!" he shouted.

"Okay, kids," Uncle Dwight said as the nine kids gathered around him.

"This is it! We're a team! Go out and play your best, and *enjoy* your first game!"

Annabelle raised her hand. "Coach Jones, you have always said that we should sing before we practice. I think we should sing before our game, too."

"What a great idea, Annabelle. What song?"

"I was thinking of our national anthem."

"Perfect," Uncle Dwight said. "Hats off for our national anthem," he boomed.

Annabelle took out her harmonica from her back pocket. Then she motioned to Margie. Margie held up a flag with a wooden stick. She held it high in the air.

"Hmmmmm." Annabelle sounded the first note, and then she began to play the entire anthem. Everyone who could remember the words sang:

"Oh say can you see,
By the dawn's early light,
What so proudly we hailed
At the twilight's last gleaming.
Whose broad stripes and bright stars,
Through the perilous fight,
O'er the ramparts we watched,
Were so gallantly streaming?
And the rockets' red glare,
The bombs bursting in air,
Gave proof through the night
That our flag was still there.
Oh say does that star-spangled
Banner yet wave
O'er the land of the free
And the home of the brave?"

"Play ball!" Uncle Dwight called out as his team ran out to their positions.

All except one.

Raymond walked.

Uncle Dwight noticed right away. "Hey, Captain Hustle, where are your GO! GO! GO!s?"

Ray shrugged as he walked out to right field.

Herbie looked over at his buddy from center

field. Herbie knew what was wrong. Ray was thinking about fourth grade.

"Try to forget it, Ray," Herbie called. "Maybe we can do something about it the thirteenth."

"YEAH SURE!" Ray shouted back. But he didn't seem to believe it any more.

The first Beechwood player hit a hard line drive to John Greenweed at second. John bobbled it once, then picked it up and threw it to first base.

Annabelle stretched to make the catch.

John breathed better after that first out.

"WAY TO GO ANNABELLE AND JOHN GREENWEED!" Herbie yelled. He knew he had to do Ray's rooting. The team needed enthusiasm.

The second Beechwood player hit a high pop-up into the infield. John Greenweed came in for it. "I GOT IT!" he shouted. Everyone else backed off.

"TWO OUTS!" Uncle Dwight yelled.

All the Laurel Woods kids held up two fingers.

The third batter poked the ball into center field. Herbie knew it was his. The ball was coming right to him. He remembered his dad's words, "Get ready!"

Herbie held his glove up high. He kept his eye

on that ball till it dropped in his glove. Just like Olivia and his dad showed him—squeeze the ball, squeeze the orange.

PLOP!

Herbie squeezed his glove tight, and then he put his other hand over his glove just to be safe.

"OUT!" shouted the umpire.

Mr. Jones clapped his hands. "That's my boy!"

Olivia jumped in the air. "THAT'S MY BROTHER!"

Mrs. Jones stood up in the stands and waved the laurel flower poster up and down.

Herbie peeked in the glove. He couldn't believe the ball was in there. IT WAS!

He leaped in the air. "I DID IT!"

Annabelle came right over to Herbie and patted him on the back. "Good catch, Herb Jones."

"All right!" Phillip said as he slapped Herbie five.

The game was scheduled for six innings. For the first three, the score was 0-0. Both teams played good defense.

In the fourth inning, the Beechwood players went ahead with two runs.

Now in the bottom of the sixth inning, the score was still 2-0. This was Laurel Woods' last chance to score runs.

Herbie took his "Laurel Beef" hat off and wiped his forehead. He looked at the roster. It was the bottom of the batting order—Margie Sherman and Herbie Jones.

Uncle Dwight called his team over, "Okay, kids, you've been playing great defense. We have a chance to even the score. Let's not give up now!"

The team watched Margie hit the ball into center field.

"She got a double! We're in this game!" Uncle Dwight shouted.

Margie waved from second base. "GO LAUREL WOODS!" she yelled.

It was Herbie's turn at the plate.

Uncle Dwight moved behind the backstop with Mr. Jones. "Come on, Herbie," he said. "Pretend that sun is the moon and hit the ball the way you did that night we were practicing."

"You did it before," Olivia called, "you can do it again."

Herbie remembered. He remembered those two balls he hit well into the field. Forget the other eighty-eight. He hit two well. He *could* do it.

"This guy struck out twice before. I'll take him again," the pitcher called out.

The pitcher hurled a fastball across the plate. Herbie swung and missed.

"Strike one," the umpire called.

As the pitcher wound up, Herbie watched the ball. He concentrated. He concentrated like he did with his dad when they were tossing that orange back and forth while the kettle was shrilling.

Herbie got a small corner of the next pitch. It fouled off into the bleachers.

"Strike two," the umpire said.

"YOU GOT A PIECE!" Uncle Dwight called. "You're up with the ball."

"You can do it!" a voice replied from the bench. Herbie looked up. It was Phillip McDoogle.

The pitcher threw Herbie a high ball.

He went after it early.

CRACK!

It zoomed into right field!

Herbie took off for first base like he was the Roadrunner himself.

Everyone jumped off the bench and cheered. Margie scored while Herbie was safe at first base. He got his first hit in a game!

Uncle Dwight hugged Mr. Jones. Mrs. Jones hugged Mrs. Martin.

Shadow raced back and forth barking.

"It's 2-1. We're in this game!" shouted Uncle Dwight.

Annabelle Louisa Hodgekiss was now at the plate. It was the top of the batting order. She took out her batting gloves and smoothed them over her fingers. She did some knee bends and deep breathing exercises. She stretched the bat high above her head and made several twists. After she tapped the dirt from her cleats, she took her batting stance.

"I'm ready," she called.

The pitcher motioned for his players to move back. "She's a hitter."

He pitched the first ball over the plate.

Annabelle just watched it.

"Strike one!" the umpire said.

"That was so low night crawlers could have gotten it," Mr. Hodgekiss complained behind the backstop.

He was still wearing his flowered apron but he was standing next to Mr. Jones and the coach now.

Annabelle lined up her knuckles.

The pitcher threw a high ball. Annabelle went for it.

"BLAM!" Annabelle ripped the ball into center field.

Herbie rounded second. Then he rounded third. Just as he came across the plate to tie the score, the people in the bleachers jumped to their feet and clapped.

Mr. Hodgekiss tore off his apron and threw it in the air.

It landed on Shadow who was barking loudly.

"It's 2-2! We have a tie ball game with Annabelle at third!" Uncle Dwight shouted.

Annabelle held up three fingers. "I got a triple, Dad!" she yelled.

Mr. Hodgekiss waved back. "Way to go, Annie."

"Who's up?" Phillip asked. "We have a chance to win this game. We just have to bring Annabelle home."

Everyone looked at the coach.

"Ray Mart's up," Uncle Dwight replied.

But where was he?

He was buying a chili dog at the refreshment stand.

"GET OVER HERE, RAY MART!" Uncle Dwight bellowed. "We need your big bat."

Herbie ran over to his buddy. "You can do it, Ray Mart. You got on twice before with your blasts to third base."

Ray finished his chili dog in three bites. "Yeah, okay."

Herbie knew Ray had lost his interest in baseball. He was too busy thinking bad thoughts about fourth grade.

And then just as Ray Mart took the plate, Miss Pinkham came running down the park pathway. "Sorry I'm late," she called.

Ray looked up and made a face.

Herbie was worried.

Ray was really distracted now. Would it interfere with his hitting?

Herbie took out his notepad. He looked at the words next to number one and number three—enthusiasm and Don't give up!

Herbie immediately started a chant, "GO RAY MART! GO RAY MART!"

The rest of the team joined in, "GO RAY MART! GO RAY MART!"

"Back up, you guys," the Beechwood pitcher said. "This guy is a hitter, remember?"

The pitcher hurled the ball.

Ray took a golf swing at it.

"Strike one," the umpire said.

Herbie sat down on the bench. Ray was going back to his old style of hitting. The team was in big trouble.

"Level swing," Herbie shouted from the bench. "GO RAY MART!" he chanted again.

"GO RAY MART!" the team chimed in.

The pitcher threw Ray another ball.

This time Ray connected.

But it was a nubber.

"GO!" shouted Uncle Dwight as Ray took off for first. "GO!" Uncle Dwight repeated as he waved Annabelle home.

It was going to be close.

Everyone who had moved back now rushed forward.

The catcher squatted at the plate and waited.

Annabelle ran so fast her hat flew off and her pigtails waved in the wind.

The shortstop finally got the ball and threw it home.

Annabelle was only a yard away.

The ball was in the air now.

Annabelle slid home.

And in the pile of smoke dust, the umpire leaned over to make the call. "SAFE!"

The entire Laurel Woods team jumped off the bench and raced for homeplate. "WE WON!" they shouted.

Everyone made a long line and took turns shaking Annabelle's hand. Shadow was at the end barking.

"Now," Herbie exclaimed, "let's get the nubber king! After all, he's the one who got the winning hit!"

The team raced for first base and lifted Ray into the air.

"You said it first, Ray!" Herbie replied. "We're baseball greats!"

But Raymond didn't hear Herbie. The chanting was too loud—"RAY MART! RAY MART! RAY MART!"

14

July 13th—The Wedding

Herbie and Ray hid behind the bushes of the Center Church and waited for the wedding party. It was 3:45 P.M.

"I don't know why you insisted on bringing the Monster Ball," Herbie said.

"It's our secret weapon. It has great power. This is the most important spy mission of our lives, Herbie. We need the Monster Ball with us."

Herbie pushed a branch away from his face. "Ray, my uncle is the only one who really knows what the Monster Ball says. I just ordered a pickle for him once."

"Oh," Ray said as he tucked the Monster Ball under his arm. "What kind?"

Herbie jabbed Raymond. "Here they come! Quick, let's duck into the church and sit in the last row."

Herbie followed Ray as he raced inside the blue door and quickly found a safe seat in the last pew.

"Look!" Ray whispered. "There's Miss Pinkham."

"Shh!" Herbie replied. "We don't want her to see us." And then he added, "Who's that lady with the flowers behind her?"

"Probably one of her birdmaids," Raymond suggested.

"Birdmaids? You mean bridesmaids," Herbie corrected.

"You're right," Ray agreed. "I never saw one of those ladies fly off."

Herbie made a face.

Then they saw Uncle Dwight down by the altar with the minister and another guy.

"Gee," Ray said, "his shirttail is even tucked in. And his hair is combed!"

"Miss Pinkham sure looks pretty," Herbie commented. "She has flowers in her hair."

The boys watched the minister. He was holding a Bible.

They saw him step forward to recite the vows.

"Something's wrong," Herbie said as he watched the ceremony.

"I know," Ray agreed. "They shouldn't be getting married. Be ready to speak right up!"

"No, dummy. Look at the couple standing in front of the minister. It's not Uncle Dwight and Miss Pinkham. Miss Pinkham is standing to the left of the other lady. Uncle Dwight is standing to the right of the other guy."

"Huh?" Ray stood up. When he did, the Monster Ball slipped from under his arm, rolled along the pew seat and bounced out into the middle of the aisle.

"Oh, no, our secret weapon," Ray whispered.

"I'll take care of it," Herbie said. "You keep your eyeballs on the ceremony. Something's funny about it."

"Right on," Ray said as he made binoculars out of his fists.

Herbie looked at the Monster Ball. It was staring at the altar. Herbie knew it would be greeting the bride and groom when they came back up the aisle.

Herbie HAD to get it.

He dropped to his knees and crawled along the red carpet to the edge of the pew. Reaching his hand out as far as he could, he tried to get the ball

back, but instead the Monster Ball just rolled far-
ther away.

Herbie got an idea. He lurched out from the
pew and kicked the Monster Ball into the lobby.

Then he followed it and ducked around the corner.

"Is this THING yours?" a voice said.

Herbie looked up. There was Annabelle Louisa
Hodgekiss holding the Monster Ball. She was
wearing a long white dress, a white bonnet and
white lace gloves.

"Are you getting married, too?" Herbie asked.

"Don't be silly, Herbie Jones," Annabelle said,
shoving the Monster Ball in his arms. "I just happened to be in the neighborhood. I'm on my way
to Price Busters to get my mother a quart of milk."

"Dressed like that?"

Annabelle ignored the question. "Shh! I want to
watch the rest of the wedding."

Just then Ray came dashing into the lobby.

"Herbie, they got married!"

"*Who* got married?" Herbie remembered Uncle
Dwight and Miss Pinkham were on the *outside* of
the other couple.

Annabelle put her hands on her hips. "Miss Pinkham and your uncle, dummy."

Ray looked at Annabelle and then took a step back. He could hardly keep himself from laughing. Quickly he pulled Herbie aside. "That *birdmaid* married the *other guy!*"

"You sure?" Herbie said.

Ray was talking to both Herbie and Annabelle now. "Yeah. They gave each other rings and then they did the K word."

Herbie dropped the Monster Ball and cringed.

Annabelle flared her nostrils. "I missed the best part, thanks to you and that thing." She pointed to the Monster Ball.

Herbie and Ray jumped in the air and slapped each other ten.

Annabelle shook her head. "I thought you boys *didn't* want Miss Pinkham to get married."

"She didn't," Herbie replied as he picked up the Monster Ball and ran down the church steps three at a time.

"YAHOO! Wait for me!" Ray called.

Annabelle quickly grabbed Ray's shirttail. "Just a minute. I need an explanation. Isn't Miss Pinkham a bride?"

Raymond turned. "No, she's a birdmaid."

"A birdmaid? What in the world is a birdmaid?" Annabelle shouted.

"If you let go of my shirt, I'll tell you."

Annabelle let go.

Raymond grinned. "Nanny nanny nah nah!" And then he ran away laughing until he caught up with Herbie and the Monster Ball.

Annabelle was so mad she stamped her foot and screamed, "RAYMOND MARTIN AND HER-BIE JONES, YOU ARE BOTH *BIRDBRAINS*!"

Herbie and Raymond skipped ahead, flapping their elbows. "Chirp! Chirp! Chirp! Chirp!" they called out as they took turns bouncing the Monster Ball home.